Cantsee

The Cat Who Was
the Color of the Carpet

Cantsee

The Cat Who Was
the Color of the Carpet

WRITTEN AND ILLUSTRATED BY

Gretchen Schields

Gulliver Books
Harcourt Brace & Company
SAN DIEGO   NEW YORK   LONDON

Requests for permission to make copies of any part of the work should be mailed to:
Permissions Department, Harcourt Brace & Company, 6277 Sea Harbor Drive,
Orlando, Florida 32887-6777.

Gulliver Books is a registered trademark of Harcourt Brace & Company.

Library of Congress Cataloging-in-Publication Data
Schields, Gretchen.
Cantsee: the cat who was the color of the carpet/
written and illustrated by Gretchen Schields.—1st ed.
p. cm.
"Gulliver Books."
Summary: Mr. Blue takes in a homeless kitten as a pet but keeps losing track of the
animal as he blends in perfectly with his surroundings.
ISBN 0-15-200547-1
[1. Cats—Fiction. 2. Camouflage (Biology)—Fiction.
3. Stealing—Fiction.] I. Title.
PZ7.S3455Can 1996
[Fic]—dc20 95-18988

First edition
A B C D E

Printed in Singapore

The illustrations in this book were done in Dr. Martin dyes, watercolor,
and ink on cold-press, double-weight Crescent illustration board.
The display type was set in Rogers.
The text type was set in Clearface.
Color separations were made by Bright Arts, Ltd., Singapore.
Printed and bound by Tien Wah Press, Singapore
This book was printed with soya-based inks on Leykam recycled paper,
which contains more than 20 percent postconsumer waste and
has a total recycled content of at least 50 percent.
Production supervision by Warren Wallerstein and Pascha Gerlinger
Designed by Kaelin Chappell

For Jake

EVERY DECEMBER people lined up around the block to see the unusual holiday windows of the grand Le Blue Mercantile Emporium department store. Mr. Blue, the store owner, had decorated the windows as miniature rooms, with animal-size furniture, tiny Christmas trees, chew-bones, and catnip mice. In each little room, puppies and kittens played.

All the furry creatures needed new homes. With these enchanting windows, the Homeless Creatures Society and kindly Mr. Blue had created a popular way to attract families that might adopt the pets.

It was late one night. Outside, a sliver of a moon was rising. Inside the store, Mr. Blue whistled happily to himself. Today all the little ones had found new families.

Mr. Blue finished tidying up the windows for the next day. As he straightened the carpet in the very last window, he felt the tug of a small claw on his trousers leg.

"What's this?" Mr. Blue wondered, looking down at his feet. The patterns in the Persian carpet wiggled a bit. Peering closer, Mr. Blue discovered a tiny kitten. "Were you left behind, little fellow?" asked Mr. Blue. "It's no wonder! You blend right into the rug. Why, I can hardly see you!"

Mr. Blue scooped up the tiny cat, who stared at him intently. "Aah, I'll have to take you home tonight myself," said Mr. Blue. The kitten purred loudly. Mr. Blue tucked the kitten into the pocket of his overcoat, locked the big front doors of the store, and set off for home.

Mr. Blue lived in a fanciful Victorian home cluttered with many strange and curious things. He unlocked his front door and put the kitten down. The kitten scampered into the house and promptly disappeared into the Christmas tree. Mr. Blue looked around at the bric-a-brac, the antimacassars, and the Chinese vases.

"Oh, dear," sighed Mr. Blue. "Perhaps this was a mistake. I wonder if I shall ever find him again. A vanishing cat! A cat the color of the carpet. A cat I can't see!"

Mr. Blue took off his glasses and polished them with his pocket handkerchief. "Well, that's what I'll call him if he ever turns up again," he said, setting the spectacles back on his nose. "Yes, that's the name for him— Cantsee the cat! But where can he be hiding?"

The branches of the Christmas tree waved frantically. Between a crystal angel and a blown-glass pig, the furry face of Cantsee peeked up at Mr. Blue. "What a little scamp," murmured Mr. Blue as Cantsee lost his grip amid the branches and tumbled to the floor, where he disappeared immediately into the patterns of the Turkish rug. "You're going to keep me on my toes!"

Mr. Blue decided to settle in and enjoy the evening paper. He unfolded it on the table. "Let's see what the news of the world is tonight," he said to himself, studying the page before him. The letters were jumbled and hard to read. Sentences stopped in the middle and picked up elsewhere. He rubbed his eyes. *Do I need new spectacles?* he wondered. From the open page came an insistent "Miaow!"

Cantsee! Peering closer, Mr. Blue was able to make out the kitten, stretched happily across the newspaper. He reached out and thoughtfully stroked the furry page. It broke out in grateful purring. "This magically changing cat needs pinning down. He'll drive me crazy," Mr. Blue mused.

Then Mr. Blue had an idea. With the kitten in hand, he found a bell and tied it on a ribbon around Cantsee's neck. But this only confused things more, for Cantsee shook himself noisily, jumped through the strings of Mr. Blue's harp, and toppled his music box aviary. This set off all the mechanical birds at once, and the sound of Cantsee's bell was lost in a musical riot of cheeping and piping and tinkling. "Oh dear!" exclaimed Mr. Blue. "Now he's vanishing into sounds as well."

At teatime Mr. Blue made himself a sardine sandwich. But before he could take a bite, half of the sandwich disappeared from his plate. Cantsee had come and gone. Mr. Blue made himself another sandwich and poured cream into his teacup. It seemed to be disappearing into the bottom of the cup. Suddenly a furry ball inside the teacup uncurled itself, stretched, and licked his hand. Cantsee jumped out of the teacup and vanished into the swirls of Mr. Blue's lace napkin.

Mr. Blue, who had led a quiet life up till now, was tired out by all of Cantsee's tricks. He looked around one last time for the provocative kitten and, not finding him, went to bed. Mr. Blue did not see the little cat pad hopefully after him across the tile floor, scamper up the carpeted stairs, and finally leap onto the bed to curl up at his feet on the counterpane.

The next morning before leaving for Le Blue Mercantile Emporium, Mr. Blue considered the situation. How was he going to live with a kitten who kept disappearing into all of the clutter and patterns of his house? Then he reluctantly went to the telephone and called one of his friends. "This kitten is just not happy with me!" he told the friend. "He hides from me all the time. And then he jumps out at me from the wallpaper! Perhaps he'd be happier in your home."

The friend, who lived in an uncluttered modern house that had white floors and solid-colored walls with no nooks or crannies, agreed to take Cantsee. He had been wanting a cat to eat the bugs that occasionally wandered in. Mr. Blue promised to take the kitten to him the very next day.

The foliage in the solarium rustled alarmingly as Cantsee listened to this conversation from his perch among the plants. The kitten emerged from the anthuriums and caladiums and shook himself all over. He didn't want to be sent away! This was the only real home he'd ever had. What would change Mr. Blue's mind? How could Cantsee prove to Mr. Blue what a worthwhile, if unusual, companion he could be? Cantsee thought and thought, and then had an idea. Gifts! He would win Mr. Blue over with gifts of love. Cantsee jumped out the window and disappeared into the garden to find Mr. Blue the perfect present.

That evening when he returned home from the store, Mr. Blue went to put on his carpet slippers and found a mouse in one. "EEEEEK!" he screamed, and quickly put his shoes back on. The mouse fled from the toe of the slipper, where Cantsee had put it, and scooted out the door. Cantsee followed to seek a different treat, one that Mr. Blue might like better.

Mr. Blue mopped his brow with his pocket handkerchief and sat down heavily in his chair. He breathed in the fresh air from the open window. Suddenly six wiggling night crawlers appeared in the window. They were seemingly suspended in thin air, for Cantsee, now the color of the starry night sky, held them in his mouth. Mr. Blue gasped in alarm and slammed the window shut. The earthworms fell back into the garden and Cantsee tumbled inside.

Silhouetted against the stars, Cantsee pressed his nose against the cold windowpane and gazed mournfully out at the dark night. Mr. Blue had certainly seen the gifts, but he hadn't seen the *giver*. Cantsee watched his rejected slippery gifts crawl back into their holes. The little cat dropped without a sound onto the rug and vanished into its paisley patterns to await his fate. If he *couldn't* be seen, he *wouldn't* be seen. He was a kitten, after all, and one who could disappear at will.

All the surprises had given Mr. Blue a headache, so he warmed a toddy for himself and took it off to bed. He inspected his bed, shaking the quilt and fluffing the pillows, in case more kitten gifts were waiting for him there. No loathsome things appeared to have been deposited by a misguided kitten. Mr. Blue sighed in relief. He would find that Cantsee in the morning and give him away as a Christmas present to his friend.

The next day was Christmas Eve, and Mr. Blue's house was strangely still when he awoke. There were no more raids on the tea tray, no more gifts of mice or worms. Mr. Blue looked under the Christmas tree. There was no kitten among the presents. He carefully inspected the pages of his stamp collection. He saw no kitten bearing the postmark of a foreign land. Mr. Blue picked up each and every porcelain shepherdess in his china cabinet and turned her over, but there was no kitten among them masquerading as a lamb. All morning Cantsee watched Mr. Blue search but sat still as a stone on the rug.

After several hours of searching, Mr. Blue sat down to rest. He scratched his head and asked, "How can one miss a cat who one could never see anyway? But I do!" Mr. Blue reached for the telephone and called his friend. "I can't find that kitten anywhere. And I may wish to reconsider giving him up. I actually may wish to *keep* him. That is, if I still have him!" Cantsee pondered this development but kept his own counsel.

As Mr. Blue sat in his chair wondering if he was ever going to find Cantsee again (and if he couldn't, what would he do), he heard a thump on the roof. Could it be Santa? More likely, it was that little cat with some new trick in store for him! But before he could even get up from his armchair to investigate, two intruders surprised Mr. Blue mightily by sliding down his chimney and emerging from between the Christmas stockings hung from the mantel.

The burglars tied Mr. Blue to the chair and went to work. Into their sacks they threw ormolu clocks, Chinese locks, silver salvers and strings of pearls, chandeliers and bandoliers and lavalieres, the golden crown of Tutankhamen, Balinese masks and rumba drums. . . . The fun had just begun! The thieves whooped happily as they helped themselves to everything in sight. "Oh, dear. Oh, dear," lamented Mr. Blue. He struggled in vain against his bonds as he watched the thieves pillage his house.

From his hiding place, Cantsee, the cat who was the color of the carpet, watched, too. Then a patch of paisley in the rug began to tremble and blur around the edges. A tail emerged, the fur standing up stiffly in outrage.

The tail switched like a whip. Two eyes narrowed
and glinted steely silver. Whiskers twitched.
A cat—a very angry cat—hissed into focus.

Cantsee tensed and sprang
from the arabesques
of the rug into the
face of one of the thugs.
The thief shouted in alarm as sharp little claws scratched his face. He hadn't
seen anything coming! With lightning speed, Cantsee flew, snarling like the
wind, at the other thief and bit his ear, then back at the first, claws slashing.

Mr. Blue stopped struggling and watched in amazement. He saw a little cat
erupt from a Picasso painting of a woman's nose. He saw a furious kitten
jump out of the clock in the
stomach of a bronze mermaid.
Mr. Blue could see him clearly!
The jaw on the suit of armor
clanged open and Cantsee leaped
out, scratching at the terrified
thieves. Mr. Blue watched
as the intruders screamed
and swatted blindly at the
ghostly demon.

At last the baffled burglars dropped their sacks and fled from the haunted house and its invisible avenger, out the French doors and into the night. Cantsee watched them disappear, then turned and walked quite visibly across the rug to Mr. Blue. The two regarded each other solemnly.

"You *can* be seen!" exclaimed Mr. Blue. "And I can see you!"

With the help of Cantsee's teeth and claws, Mr. Blue was soon free of the ropes. Mr. Blue beamed fondly at Cantsee. "We'll be together happily ever after! I'll certainly not send *you* away." Then he pulled out his pocket handkerchief and spread it on the rug. "You don't have to be seen if you don't want to be, though I'd certainly like to see you once in a while," Mr. Blue said with a laugh. "And here's a special place for you to go when you *want* to be seen!"

Cantsee sauntered across the rug and sat, half on, half off the white handkerchief. Cantsee, the cat who was the color of the carpet, licked his whiskers proudly, half of him glimmering and blending into the patterns of the rug, the other half beautifully visible and glowing bright white on Mr. Blue's handkerchief. Then Mr. Blue scooped up Cantsee and hugged him close. Cantsee purred happily, and as he snuggled into Mr. Blue's arms, his color turned bright, bright blue.